What Lies Beyond, Within

from the author,
DAVID BARTO,
to SCOTT SIMON,
in appreciation for all you
do on "Weekend Edition."
I hope that my short offering
returns some of the Positive
moments you gave to me from and
on NPR over the years.
My Heavenly Father gave me
this view of our future that
I share with you:
His message is
mine, that LOVE,
which God is,
is the image we
are made in, and
the most
important
element of our
universe,
yesterday, today,
and forever.

David Monroe Barto

May 20th, 2025

ISBN 979-8-88540-134-0 (paperback)
ISBN 979-8-88540-135-7 (digital)

Christian Faith Publishing
832 Park Avenue
Meadville, PA 16335
www.christianfaithpublishing.com

Printed in the United States of America

Where there is love there is life.

—Mahatma Gandhi

Love is the answer to everything.
It's the only reason to do anything.

—Ray Bradbury

Love doesn't make the world go round.
Love is what makes the ride worthwhile.

—Elizabeth Barrett Browning

God is love.
Let us make Man in our image, after our likeness.
You shall love the Lord your God.
You shall love your neighbor as yourself.
Love never ends.
By this all men will know that you are my
disciples, if you have love for one another.

—The Holy Bible in 1 John 4:8, Genesis 1:26,
Matthew 22:37–39, 1 Corinthians 13:4, John 13:35

You will know the truth, and the truth will make
you free... I am the way, and the truth,
and the life.

—Jesus of Nazareth in John 8:32,14:6

Galileo Statue by John Massey Rhind, 1907
Carnegie Museum of Natural History, Pittsburgh, Pennsylvania

Prologue

I have been to the future—not a fictional, imagined place, mind you, but to the real thing. I know how things really end up, so to speak, by a certain time. In many science fiction works, in short stories, novels and movies, the future looks like the kind of place to which I would be fortunate to escape. Technology has made life easier. Space exploration has given more options of where to live, for where to have adventures, for where to find more resources, and there is less use of an overworked planet earth and more use of the sun. And in some more pessimistic views, we have let ourselves down and live in a postwar apocalyptic ruin of an earth where characters walk uneventfully through the dramatic ruins of New York City, of Paris, of London, of what once was a thriving planet environment. They might recognize the top half of the fallen Statue of Liberty or what remains of Big Ben or the Eiffel Tower.

I saw that those visual human-made relics of the present world are gone in the next chapter of our kind. Our race's future is disturbing in one profound, tragic way, and hopeful in another. The disturbing view is the moral depravity that has lead humans to live for the fabricated titillation of their emotions and thoughts. This central selfish focus has been at the sacrifice of human interaction, of friendship, of love, of meaningful, constructive social relationships. We have become lonely, autonomous souls living for the next artificial thrill but not by using drugs, which would have been my guess, looking at our present interests. That surprised me.

There have been great advances in technology, but that is not the hopeful part of the future I saw. For that, I give you my personal account of what is to come. You may see it for yourself. Granted, no two eyes view the same world identically and necessarily draw the same conclusions, even if what I claim to be is, in fact, the actual true view of the future. But I will do my best for you.

I can say this, at least, that you will be looking through the correct window into the world that is to come. For that you can trust me and, more importantly, may draw up the blinds to make your own conclusions. Be forewarned by what you are about to read. The future may not be as bright and optimistic as you might hope.

Life Chapter 1

The Fateful Run

It was not long ago that I was walking the streets of Pittsburgh, very much looking forward to weeks of summer vacation, time off from the intensity of campus life at a school to the north of the city. I had spent a leisurely day visiting my favorite place, the Natural History Museum. I closed the large door behind and descended the moonlit steps, pulling up my collar to the chilly breezes. I walked down Forbes Avenue, into the night, moving toward the Greyhound bus station several miles away.

My thoughts were integrated with purpose, having been greatly refreshed and newly directed by my three years of study. I attended a Christian school because it complemented my faith. Yet there loomed an unexplained emptiness inside me. I had been praying for some sign that where my education major was taking me was best for my future and where God needed me in the world. However, with no answer to my constant pleas for a year, I was facing a crisis of faith and wondering if God was really listening or maybe was even there at all, whether what Professor Manning had said was possibly true, that to the world, the whole God concept was just what some young people needed after leaving home, just an extension of the parental relationship for adults. I was really confused now. Was it possible that humans need such an imagined figure of authority and love to keep it together in this world, so we invent a father figure like God to help keep us balanced? Were my years of church attendance a waste? Was

I naive to believe what my Sunday school teachers explained about what Jesus did for us on the cross, or was it really a myth? How do I approach the possibility that I was duped into my faith? Not an easy thing to think about.

I looked up to heaven and thought, *Are you really there, God? If so, please convince me by helping me with this dilemma.* Ironically, I walked past the Galileo sculpture next to the museum. With his head supported by the fingers of his left hand, Galileo seemed to be in the same thought about the meaning of life as I was. I wish I knew what answer that great mind had found. It might help me now.

Unthinking, I instinctively lifted someone's garbage can and lid from the street and paused, wondering at this random act of unconscious good. Could such kindness prove that we are created in the image of a loving, caring God? Maybe the problem was that I thought about things too much. Yes. This was getting boring, and much too deep. Maybe I just needed to focus on the blocks left to get to the bus station and on sleeping the long six-hour trip across Pennsylvania to visit friends near Philadelphia. What would I do this summer that was fun?

I plunged my numbing hands into my warm coat pockets and considered the old city sites I passed. In the moonlight, the old row houses and littered sidewalk and street made me suddenly somewhat fearful for my safety in the night. Smiling children had been playing there when I had passed earlier; but this quiet darkness invited fear, as did that quiet darkness of faith inside me, and my forlorn hope that God would answer my prayer to let me know that He was really there. "Please be there, God. I need you. Please be real," I whispered as I looked up to the dark sky once again.

I jumped suddenly as an unworldly scream tore through the icy stillness! It was a girl's voice. I automatically dashed down the nearest alleyway toward that desperate sound, dodging overflowing street cans, soggy, torn plastic bags losing trash, trying to run through a sea of junk. I lost my footing on a wave of beer cans and plastic and glass bottles and fell headfirst into a heap of foul-smelling, soft goo. As I tried to get back onto my feet, a savage-faced dog leaped at me from a back doorway. I buried my head as the beast extended its leash. The chain crackled as the collar bit into the dark neck and pulled back angry, snapping jaws! Sliding carefully out of reach, I got up, wiping the globs of saliva-like drippings from my face and coat arm. I moved on toward the closer, louder, continuing screams, leaving the barking demon behind.

Rounding a corner and taking a moment to catch my breath and to get accustomed to new surroundings, I found myself across the street from a park. I stared in disbelief as I made out the figure of a screaming girl, not fifty yards away, moving wildly on her back, her wrists being held firmly down to the grass by a laughing, hooded figure, working his body savagely atop hers to keep her under control. His guttural laughs mixed with the hysterical moans and desperate cries for help of the writhing girl.

"Oh, God! Someone, please help me! Get off of me, you loser! Get off of me now!"

"Haha! Or you'll do what, girlie girl? Why don't you relax and enjoy the moment? I'm sure gonna enjoy this ride. I'm gonna make your day. Haha!"

I added my shout to the confusion. "Hey, you! Get offa her!"

A greasy, dirty face reflected in the night light as it turned toward me and snarled, "Yeah? Or you're gonna do exactly what about it, you young punk? Get outa here, or I'll kick your ass! You're ruinin' my fun."

Clouds passed quickly by the moon and hid the sight, encouraging me to move toward the scene as I was hidden for a moment by the brief darkness. I thought how I was asking for trouble, how maybe doing the commonsense thing was to turn around and to head back down the alley and leave. But it wasn't in my nature to let the girl down, leaving her to the whims of her captive. I rushed the laughing hooded enemy as he turned back to his victim.

I saw a flash of steel as the moonlight reappeared, as I kicked the hooded head with all my might. I was a soccer player, and the kick was natural and with decided force. My only regret in the action was that I was just too late and that the maniac had time to hit home with the blade as the girl let out one more scream and grew still after a loud moan!

The momentum from my running kick rolled me past the two as I fell. I looked back and noticed the hoped-for effect as the collapsed hooded figure several times clutched and released his now hidden head and cried out, "Dammit! Who the hell do you think you are? You coulda killed me, you punk!" The lunatic gave me a menacing stare as he stood up, made a stumbling turn and disappeared into the darkness, knife still drawn by his side, mumbling about how someone had ruined his damn fun.

Despite the huge pain in my foot, I was able to limp over to the now lifeless form the madman had left behind. I pulled her dark hair aside and found her eyes were still open. I was stunned by the contrast of the now quiet, seemingly peaceful night as moonlight reflected the girl's horror-stricken expression. Her obviously pretty face was now distorted by the act of a murderous fiend. Her eyes closed, and I lifted her wrist and was rewarded by the faint trace of a heartbeat. I held her hand between both of mine and looked up to heaven, thinking, *Oh, God. Please help. Why does a god who is supposed to be love allow things like this to happen?*

I heard some windows opening. A man's angry voice came at me. "Hey, you! Get away from that girl. You leave her alone. I called the police. I hope they kick your ass." A female voice added, "Henry! Hush! You'll wake up the whole city."

I tried to call back through tear-drenched eyes and choking thoughts that I wasn't the one who hurt the girl and would he also call for an ambulance, but my quivering mouth could not get out the words my lips formed. I looked down, and the girl had regained consciousness for a moment. There was a trace of appreciation in her faint smile. She tried to speak, and I leaned forward and barely detected a faint whisper: "Thank you," she said. She weakly motioned toward her waist. I pulled up a portion of her blue blouse that was soaked blood red now and noticed the flow of red fluid from her torn abdomen. I grabbed some of her blouse, bunched it up, and pressed it down on the wound. She winced and convulsed with pain, her head rolling to the side as her eyes closed. I stood and whipped off my coat and covered her with it, pressing down once more on the makeshift bandage. More windows were opening, and people shouting things at me, about how I had better get away from the girl, about how I would get what was coming to me.

I now heard the sound of an approaching vehicle braking hard as it neared the area. I hoped that it was medical help. That moment was the first time I really noticed the entire block of tall, battered row homes along the park. I continued the constant pressure on the wound. The girl did not respond as she appeared completely unconscious now. I was thinking of what else I could do when a speeding car with flashing red lights came racing, skidding around a corner, its tires screeching to a sliding halt. Two figures leaped out, being careful to remain behind the two open front car doors. "Put your hands up!" one of them barked. There was cheering from the open windows.

"Get his ass!" someone yelled.

"Make him pay!" someone else offered.

I slowly stood up, bewildered. Now sirens were also approaching. I hastily decided I didn't have a chance to prove my innocence and turned and ran in the same direction the hooded figure had gone. A shot rang out, and my left shoulder kicked forward. I was hit! In disbelief, I clutched at the sudden pain and ran on with increasing speed, getting behind some bushes for cover. Another shot. Another, both missing, but one hitting a nearby tree. I had to get out of here!

I left behind the sound of more screeching tires, the crescendo of sirens, and the rhythmic flashing of lights on the buildings. I passed a sign that read "Phipps Conservatory and Botanical Garden." I thought, *Good. Maybe I can lose the police in the natural cover.*

The sound of people shouting faded somewhat as I got deeper into the garden. There was another sign just ahead, "Panther Hollow Run." I took it and found it to be some kind of trail. At the end was a cyclone fence, separating me in the park from what was a way of getting back into the main street. I instinctively jumped onto the fence, grabbing it, and scrambled over, collapsing into a small grouping of shrubs on the other side, next to the street. I felt safe for a moment. However, in no time, there was the sound of confusion behind me growing louder. Angry, frustrated voices of men calling to one another drew closer. A dog barked. They were after me!

The leaves under my resting body felt so soft and inviting. I was tempted to stay. Maybe they would not be able to see me hidden in this spot, on the other side of the fence. Then I heard again the barking of what must have been a police dog as someone coaxed, "Find him, Tiger! Find him. Ben, she got a scent and is on his trail again! This way! We'll get him. Good boy, Tiger!"

Having a dog on my trail settled the debate in my head of whether or not to stay where I was. No chance of hiding here now. Get running again! Now!

Despite my aching shoulder, I was able to get to my feet and moved on but was almost immediately hit by a rushing, woozy nausea. I fought to remain aware, to stay focused. I heard a loud smack and a sudden coldness hit my face with startling impact! The icy cold arrived with a mysterious green glow coming from a tunnel. Thinking I was lucky enough to have found some kind of flood drain, I leaped toward the glow to get inside and to get away. My hopes faded, however, as I was clearly losing consciousness, probably because of the loss of blood from my wet, painful shoulder. As I fell and faded, I was surprised to feel hands grabbing me from two sides and stopping my complete collapse.

"What the…" I stammered.

"We've got you, David."

"Relax, buddy."

Two different voices encouraged me. But who? In the middle of nowhere? Who were they? And how did they know my name? I could not see them as I struggled to make out images between the night darkness and the green glow of the tunnel. I drifted toward unconsciousness into the stark coldness of the night. I saw the girl's face in my mind, her eyes, her mouth as she managed her "thank you." "God, I hope they got to her in time, that my bandage helped stop enough of the blood and kept her alive. Please, God, help her to live." I drifted off in my own nagging pain, as if I was floating into the coldness of the green tunnel, as if I was being carried away.

Life Chapter 2

In Alumina at the EmoteArama

My eyes were still closed as I regained consciousness. I sensed that I was seated, slumped down over what felt like a desk of sorts. I dared not open my eyes because I feared what I might see. Wherever I was, I was surrounded by a charged atmosphere of orgasmic shouts, screams of excitement, guttural cries, yells, and ghastly shrieks! Someone had been pressing a cup over my mouth and nose and was removing it now as I took a deep breath. Just as I strained my neck sideways and opened my eyes to see who it was, the person took the cup and was leaving, carrying some sort of box with the cup hanging below it, dangling on a wire. All I saw was someone in a brown hospital-technician-looking outfit with one of those hats doctors wear in an operating room. I sure hope I had not been operated on!

I pressed my hands hard over my ears to try to block out the annoying sounds and was fortunate that as the person who had helped me left, the door closed, and the noise all but disappeared. It was then I realized that I was in a booth. Despite the thin-looking glass windows, it was soundproof. Relief! But where the heck was I?

I stood to look around. I seemed to feel fine as my head cleared. But what I saw before me was incomprehensible! My booth was in a huge domed auditorium that had the appearance of a hospital because all the walls and ceiling were bright white. Usually the center of attention in such a venue would be an arena overlooking some sort of contest, or stage for watching a show. Instead, there was the leisurely flow of people entering on one side of the building through a large doorway, and exiting on the other side through another doorway. The droves of people coming and going all wore khaki-colored tops and bottoms. Their shirts hung over their pants on all sides by about twelve or so inches. Lines of thin men and women wearing the same outfits shuffled along.

Instead of there being seats in what normally would be the stands of such a large auditorium, there were many levels with booths like the one I was in. I was about ten levels up. On each of about twenty total of these levels were booth after booth after booth with people lined up outside each, waiting for their turn at something. The anxious thin bodies showed a desperation to get in and were impatient for the person inside each to come out. Indeed, there were three outside my cubicle even now gesturing at me to leave! One of their faces was pressed against the door, slobbering on the glass like a sick patient. Most noticeable were marks like product codes tattooed on either their ashen foreheads or on their pale right hands, next to their wrists, never in both places. That tattoo had three lines. The top line had the appearance of a code mark as it might appear if it were scanned on a box being bought in a market. It was in black. Next was a number below that. The ones I had seen so far all began with 666. The number was in blue. Finally, on the third line, and in red, were the words *MARK OF THE BEAST* in all capital letters.

I remember reading something in the Bible in Revelation about the end-times and some kind of mark of a beast. It would be too incredible if this was a scene from the end of the world! The number on the forehead of the woman banging on my booth was 666794732. Could I be in the middle of some sort of filming of an end-times movie? Were these all actors and actresses? No, it couldn't be. There was not a camera in sight.

All the people looked exactly alike, pale, emotionless zombies shuffling around on stilted legs that seemed to be glued at the knees. Their arms mostly hung down at their sides, lifeless, and seemed to be glued at the elbows. The only difference between them was the color of their hair and eyes. There was no trace of feeling on the bony faces, unless provoked. Coming and going on the ground floor, they all looked like khaki penguins herding dutifully in and out of the building.

In each glass booth was a glistening white chair and desk. Also glistening white and lying on every desktop, if it was not on someone's head, was a metallic headset of interlaced, lightweight-appearing, flexible metal strands.

Everywhere were what appeared to be unemotional yet dedicated attendants, like the one who had just left me. They stood out from the masses as they wore what I would call tree-trunk brown clinical outfits, including the hats. They were helping the people in their khaki clothes variously needing assistance.

Just below me, there was a resisting woman who had left her booth and was being restrained by two attendants while a man ran eagerly behind them into that booth's vacated space, shut the door, and pulled the headset on with desperate anticipation. Another woman was having her torn clothing replaced. Still another, a man, appeared unconscious, as I had been, and had a cup being pressed to his mouth. That cup, too, came out of a box on a wire.

Quite remarkably, at the top of each booth there was a large sign with bold black letters on white backing. These signs variously read "first kiss," "mountain blizzard," "avalanche of death," "birth canal," "entering death," "airplane passenger free fall," "leg amputation," "valley rainbow," "ocean sunset," "roller coaster," "beaten to a pulp," "hang gliding high," "smorgasbord gluttony," "drunken stupor," "outer space float," "suicidal depression," "wedding day," "wedding night," "spousal fight," "snakebite," and on and on.

It was not easy to focus further as several zombie people at my booth were banging insistently, probably because I had not used my headset and was just standing, watching things. They were wanting me to leave so they could have their time there. I looked above to see what my sign read, "heart attack."

As best I could make out then, the place was a vast entertainment center where people could put on the headsets and experience whatever the sign above each booth claimed it offered. I had never seen anything like it, even in my worst nightmares! Or if this was not a filming, was this, in fact, a nightmare?

Something had occurred to me as I watched the attendants at work on the needy bodies. I noticed that I not only no longer had pain in my shoulder. I touched it, and it did not feel as if I had ever even been shot! True enough, both my shoulders appeared fine! How could that be? Maybe I was dreaming for certain. That would prove it!

So there was the headset lying on my booth's desk. It appeared obvious that all I had to do to experience a heart attack was to put it on. Did I really want to try it? "What a peculiar way to spend the day," I said aloud. Is this what human life has come to? Finding a thrill in a booth? Where in the universe was I now, and what exactly was going on with these humanoid creatures? If I was still on earth, what had happened to amusements, like radio, TV, the computer, going out for fun with friends, or a night of leisurely reading?

I had to make a decision. The people outside my booth were increasingly frantic with me. True enough, how often did I have such an opportunity? As grotesque a prospect as this was, it was fascinating, in a most peculiar way, to experience a heart attack. Yes, the wretches outside would have to wait their turn. I was tempted now. But did I really have the guts to try this? Reluctantly, I retook my seat and considered the headset. What could it hurt? I did not see anyone being carried out of their booths dead, just in various states of distress or unconsciousness.

"Okay, I'll try it," I said out loud. And I did, too. I actually lifted the headset and set it down hard on my skull. At first, it was as if I had instantly, dramatically entered someone else's consciousness. I heard different sounds other than those outside my booth, like in a neighborhood. There was a dog barking, moving cars, children shouting. There was an alarming tingly sensation running down my arms before an excruciating pain hit my chest and knocked me to the floor, literally. My body lay in a helpless heap while the pain pounded. I fought to take my next breath and failed. I pulled off the headset and the relief was immediate. I could breathe again! The entire alarming experience stopped! That must have been what my mother had felt when she died in our kitchen of a massive heart attack. What a sad, scary last moment on earth! I had never really appreciated what she had faced until now, and faced alone. "Poor Mom."

I had had enough. Let these desperate people get what they were clamoring for. There was nothing more here for me. Yet the temptation returned. Might I find some twisted satisfaction in any of the other booths? There were so many experiences listed on the many signs. No. I had to get out of this booth, out of this building. How did I get here in the first place? Where was this insanity? Another body pushed me out of the way as I left, bolting into the booth as he shut the door behind to find out what it was like to have a heart attack.

As I descended toward the exit, I looked at some of the other signs: "ski lift accident," "last stage stomach cancer," "surfing shark attack," "LSD overdose," "hit by a Mac truck." *No*, I thought, *what in heaven's name would possess me to want to remain in this insane asylum? A few tempting experiences to try, but what is it ultimately doing for these people? No, I will reluctantly give way to the commonsense alarm bell ringing in my head.*

As I made it down to the last several levels, I paused here and there to observe many of the freak shows these creatures were putting on. But the next sign I saw convinced me to look at no others and to head directly for the exit! A young girl had her corpse-like face pressed up against her booth pane and was kissing it. She seemed to be trying to caress me though the glass or caress whomever she thought she was with anyway. I gazed into the pale red of her terribly swollen eyes as they darted from side to side at a maddening pace. She was slobbering all over the window, and I had to turn away, unable to watch her produce more of the mess of trickling-down slime from her mouth as it opened and closed like an excited fish. Above her booth the sign read "sexual climax." I was feeling hugely sick to my stomach! Happily, it was empty, or I might have given the attendants another unsavory clean and wipe task. The exit could not come soon enough after that.

As I made it to the bottom level, I had a close call! A man had everyone's attention as he banged on the booth walls and promised, "I'll get you! I'll get you if it's the last thing I do!" He opened the door and moved at us, swinging into the waiting, ducking crowd! His headset reached the end of its wired allowance and snapped off from atop his head. Onlookers fought to get in for their experience of "rage." Cautious attendants rushed over to surround the fellow to protect the crowd as he calmed down.

Well, I had apparently survived the nightmare as I joined the departing crowd. However, I could not help fearing what I might face outside. I still did not know where I was or how I got here. Was this place even on planet earth? Could I be in hell? Could this be part of the eternal torture of being separated from God? And if it was a nightmare, which was the only thing that made sense, now would be the best time to finally wake up. Please, someone, wake me up!

One bothersome observation is that no one looked into my eyes. This was peculiar in one way, but actually made me feel more comfortable in several ways. One positive side of it was that no one seemed to be questioning who I was. I must have stood out. My skin was deeply tanned, for one thing, while all of theirs was pale white. For another, I did not have that "mark of the Beast" scan code on my forehead or hand. I also walked in a flexible, animated way, not like a robot, like everyone else. I could not possibly look like I fit in. I felt so awkward, so out of place. Yes, it was clear that no one looked at one another unless they were confronting someone in a booth. And remarkably, that was the only time they spoke to one another, when banging on a booth to get their turn at being inside. They all instinctively looked at the floor. I could only benefit from these creatures not noticing me being very different.

The last thing I saw before leaving was a huge lobby. In it a sign was flashing huge blue and red letters on both side walls. It read "ALUMINA CITY 7 EmoteArama." So I was in a city, apparently one city of at least seven? And the name of this place was Alumina. Like the words *Mark of the Beast*, and like all the words on the signs identifying the booth experiences inside, the name of the city was in only capital letters. Maybe to make it stand out.

I followed the slow-moving herd as it headed outside. If what I saw on the inside of that auditorium was unbelievable, I was not ready for what I saw as I walked outside!

Life Chapter 3

The Mysterious Note

No, I was not ready for what I found outside. What surrounded me was more than the best special effects team could have produced for a science fiction movie. And it was real! I was walking into a true city of the future! I saw where the name of the place came from. It was perfect, Alumina. I was at the top of an overlook and on all sides, spread down into a valley to the edge of mountains on all sides, were tall aluminum and glass skyscrapers and other buildings of varying heights and sizes. Over the entire valley of this city was a dome. I found out later that the dome allowed the sunlight in but acted like a pair of giant sunglasses as it filtered out tanning elements. No wonder everyone's skin was so white!

Then it hit me! Yes! The sun was low enough to be ready to set soon over one of the mountaintops. I breathed a sigh of relief. I repeated what I thought aloud. "The setting sun!" And with a moon rising over the mountains on the other side, this meant that I at least appeared to still be on the planet earth!

The EmoteArama was on that overlooking hill and was the center of attention, clearly the focus of life here. Many were approaching the amusement building from all sides and many, like me, moving away. Those coming in were surprisingly sedate compared to those I had seen inside, as if they would be plugged in at the door and charged up with their excitement and become another sort of animated creature. Those leaving were obviously drained of strength.

But where to now? No one direction looked any more promising than another. They all looked identical with their long avenues headed down into a vast valley of glass and aluminum skyscraper after skyscraper to the borders of the dome. What might the city be like on the outskirts? Were there entrances with easy access? Or maybe more like prison doors? Could I even get out once I got there? Did I want to get out? And if not, was there a place for someone like me to find refuge inside? Were there others like me here? What would life be like for me in such a city? Could I get used to this? Would I become a ghostly pale white zombie like everyone else?

Suddenly, a gong sounded. The deep blast came from what was a giant, unseen speaker system. A message followed that was everywhere, resounding down all the avenues: "Attention, citizens of Alumina, attention. It is time to honor your master. Bow down now and submit to the Beast and to his enforcer, the Dragon! Lift your mark to them now!" The city had become silent as soon as the gong had sounded. Dutifully, the shuffling masses of creatures stopped where they were, lifted upward their hands or foreheads where they had the marks, as if showing them to an eye in the sky, and then got face down in the street. They remained prostrate for about three minutes until the gong sounded again. Then they got up and resumed walking as if nothing unusual had even happened. I had remained standing the entire time, and no one seemed to take notice.

I cannot overemphasize the magnitude, the significance of what I had just witnessed. This beast was obviously a dictatorial leader who demanded extreme compliance of his subordinate masses. What penalty might I have just risked by not obeying? Yes. My mind was made up. I had to get out of this place as fast as I could. There was only one explanation. This city master must be the Beast the Bible warned would come in the end-times to take over the world. What else could all this prove?

Here and there along a perfectly paved street were what appeared to be public benches, but in the form of what I might call a pillow sofa. I decided to sit down on one to think about what to do next. As my body lowered into the bench, I was taken aback! It was quite the thing! The material it was made of gave way to feel as if it was hugging me while I sat there, certainly not the benches I was used to! It was warm and inviting. Slow, reflective music I had never heard the likes of before calmed me. It was like magical chimes blowing a soothing melody in the gentle wind. But just as I was almost completely mesmerized by those calming tones, a voice interrupted the music with a message, and what it said was frightening.

"Beware, citizen! You cannot be identified. You do not have the Alumina insignia. Beware! The militia has been alerted. Turn yourself in for inspection now, citizen! You are missing the mark of the Beast."

I instantly rolled out of the cushion and instinctively walked away, trying to blend in with the departing arena crowd as nonchalantly as I could, hoping to avoid any further notice from whatever this scary-sounding city militia was.

As I had sat down in the cushion, I had felt paper bunch up in my pants pocket behind me. Indeed, I reached back and pulled out a piece of folded white paper inviting attention. I opened it and glanced in disbelief at the message I read in clear handprint: "David, after you leave the EmoteArama, you must leave the city of Alumina immediately. Do not loiter. Your life may depend upon it. You do not have the credentials to stay. They will be after you. Walk now out of the city, toward where the sun will set, toward the valley between the two western mountains, and meet friends in the wilderness. We will find you at the edge of the nuclear fence. We rescued you from your world and are waiting to greet you and to help you. You may trust us." No one had signed the note. Instead, there was the word *FISHNET* in capital letters and a small drawing of a fish. A fish, the early symbol of the Christians! Things were looking up. Someone who knew my name, someone who understood me! My spirits instantly lifted! I had to hold myself back from doing a football end zone dance right then and there in the street. I really would have stood out then!

I lined up the broad avenue that most directly headed toward the destination described. It appeared perhaps to be a three-mile walk. What choice did I have? Apparently, I was on my way to see friends at the edge of the city. And I could not get there soon enough! I sure had a lot of questions for them to answer!

Just as I set out enthusiastically, three small gray vehicles flew silently around several corners and stopped to surround me. They floated in midair, about a foot above the city surface. The same unseen person who had spoken to me from the bench, spoke again from all three vehicles simultaneously in the same directorial voice: "Citizen! Obey my command. Be still in the name of the Beast! You are in violation of Alumina City Code 2. You do not have the mark. You may not move freely in the city without the mark. You may not do business here without the mark. You are being taken into custody for questioning!"

One man exited each of the three cars and came toward me. The three were in military outfits. I expected to be taken into one of the cars. Foolish me! All three men grasped me, one by my left underarm and shoulder, one by my right underarm and shoulder, and the third by my waist. Then all three simultaneously whisked me away into the air. The flight was swift and silent.

I thought, *Oh my, this cannot be good!*

Life Chapter 4

The Interrogation

Over the avenues we flew until we ended up in front of one of the skyscrapers. As we slowly descended, I looked down and read the sign "Supreme Headquarters, City 7, Alumina." Upon landing, I saw that citizens passing that building knelt down in subservience, acknowledging the importance of the location to them. Their knees touched the pavement, and they immediately rose again and continued on down the sidewalk. The three holding me in custody did the same before entering. They did not seem concerned that I remained standing. The movement reminded me of what I used to see in the Catholic churches as the faithful genuflected before entering a pew.

As we approached the building door, all four sides simultaneously slid open, disappearing into the building walls and appearing again behind us after we went by. Once inside, the three militia men held me once more as we flew again upward. The center of the structure was open from bottom to top. Each floor had a balcony walkway on all four sides, with hallways leading out from them. Every level had a differently colored, single-floor landing area, all on the same side. About twenty floors up, we touched down on such a platform. As it was the only red one I could make out, I could only conclude that this was a special level.

We walked down one hall and made a right turn where there was a giant park in front of us. The park took up about a quarter of the building and was over five floors tall. It must have had its base on the fifteenth floor. It was clearly on the side facing the sun. Only one gigantic outer building window looked out over the domed city horizon. We could see down into the park from our floor's balcony. Below was a rainbow bridge over a stream, vegetation surrounding a path, and cushioned benches. It seemed very peaceful. We entered a small auditorium overlooking this park. I was placed in a chair facing a row of six high wooden desks, three to the left and three to the right, with a space in the center between them. The six desks had the park view, which was behind where I sat.

Six pale judicial-looking men and women in black robes were now climbing steps and entering into their desks. When they were all seated, a voice came over the speaker, "All rise for the honorable enforcer, the Dragon of the ten cities of planet earth." I did rise dutifully with the six others. The three men guarding me were already standing on both sides and behind me. So one mystery was solved. There were ten cities.

Ascending slowly from below to fill that space between the six desks rose an imposing form. Already seated in his chair was a powerful man, easily twice the size of the others. His face was stern and had a deep brown tone, in remarkable contrast with the citizens of Alumina in general, including the pale-faced judges. He remained seated and spoke when his desk came to a stop. "I the Dragon, the enforcer of the Beast and of the ten cities of planet earth, welcome you, citizens of Alumina, over which our supreme ruler, the Lord our God, the Beast, reigns."

I almost let out an amen with the rest at the part about God being the supreme ruler, until "the Beast" was added. Something was wrong with this picture. The Lord our God, the Beast?

"Our Supreme Ruler has chosen as today's reflection for his bride of all cities, from the book of his prophet Isaiah, who was writing about our master's greatness, in chapter 45, verse 22, 'Turn to me and be saved, all the ends of the earth! For I am God, and there is no other. Let us so honor our Lord and Savior, the Beast.'"

There was another dutiful "amen" offered from all seven desks. I did not so respond as I was confused and in absolute disbelief! I did distantly recall in Revelation that the Beast that was to come did blaspheme the name of God, claiming to be God himself. As the host continued, a giant picture of a man rose up behind the desks. His frame was normal size, and he was wearing a royal-looking robe and had the appearance of a tribal leader. He wore no hat, and his hair was dark black. He had a faraway look on his tanned face and a smugness that more than suggested that he was in charge, and he emanated a confidence that all was well.

"Let us show honor with a moment of silence to the one who saved the earth from destruction during the Great War, who arose from the dead after he was assassinated by an enemy, who has directed the massive engineering repair and rejuvenation of our ten modern cities these seven years, who has provided food in abundance, amusement, and entertainment to enliven our souls and to make life worthwhile again, and who offered hope for the future of humankind. In his name, let us have a moment of silence." There was the moment of promised silence which ended with the speaker's amen.

"Amen," all but I responded.

"Today we hear an unusual case of an intruder. Will you state your name for the record intruder?" He stared down at me.

"David."

"David. We have found that you have no mark of the Beast. How do you explain this?"

"I just arrived. I guess you could call me a visitor."

"We inquire, David, from where do you come?"

"I seem to have arrived through some kind of time tunnel."

"We see. Who made this gravitational bend time relocator available for you to use?"

"They never identified themselves. I apparently passed out as I entered it, and when I regained consciousness, I was in one of the booths in that EmoteArama place."

"We inquire, David, do you not know how you arrived at the booth in EmoteArama?"

"No. I was apparently at that time tunnel transporter and was not aware of anything till I woke up in that heart attack booth in that arena. I've never been here before. This is all new to me."

"We see, David. Do you harbor any malicious intentions toward Alumina or our supreme master, our God and Savior, the Beast?"

"To be honest, I'm still confused about what is going on here. No, I have no ill will toward anyone in your city."

"Have you read our universal oath, David? Are you willing to become a citizen of one of our ten cities by receiving the mark and to worship the Beast?"

"No, I have not read this oath. I didn't even know there was one. And I don't even know where this city is exactly, let alone any of the other nine. Can I be put back in that time relocator thing and just go back to the place I came from?"

"We would risk a time-shift displacement quake if we did not know the exact moment to which to return you. No, that is not possible unless you could obtain that information from those responsible for your delivery. However, you declare you do not know them."

"No, I honestly have no idea who they were, how they knew me, or why they wanted to send me here."

"David, as you seem to be a victim of circumstances through no choice of your own free will that has made you an intruder here, and, as you harbor no ill will toward us, we will hold you in the visitor home until the New Day. You will be given a copy of the Supreme Oath to read this night. We will release you under escort at the New Day to observe the wonders of our city. At sunset, you and your escort will be retrieved by the militia and taken back to the visitor home, where you will have time to review the universal oath. In two days' time then, we decree that you will be brought back to this building to sit before us for further questioning. You will be given one more opportunity to make your allegiance to the Beast by giving loyal testimony confirming your agreement with the Supreme Oath, by receiving the mark, thereby to join us as a citizen in service and allegiance to the Beast. David, is this plan acceptable to you?"

"Yes, I would like to see more of your city and how it works and to read that oath. But what happens if I decide I cannot, in good conscience, make allegiance to this oath, this city, and follow this Beast?" I pointed up to the picture.

"The Beast is our God and Savior, not a person."

Everyone responded, "Amen."

The host continued, "We will reach a decision when we meet with you again in two days and after further questioning. Just now, David, we anticipate the best for you and look with hope to your joining us in becoming a citizen of one of our ten cities, in the name of our master, the Beast. Amen."

"Amen," responded all those present except me.

"We dismiss you now, David."

I looked around and stood up when approached by the same three militia men who had escorted me in. They took me to the landing platform and floated me down to the first floor. I suspected that whatever bending was done with gravitation to go from one time to another, must be the same principle they had mastered that allowed them to float so easily around the city and in this building. However, none of the citizens did anything but appear to walk here and there. But I found out later that I was wrong. Citizens had a matter transporter where they could send themselves to another transporter anywhere in the ten cities. I could not use it, though, since it operated after identifying the mark tattoo on the citizen's hand or forehead.

As the building doors closed behind us and we walked out into the avenue area again, I heard a familiar sound. It was the gong announcing the simultaneous moment of demonstrable worship of the masses. As before, the citizens showed the marks on their right hands or foreheads to the sky, then fell prostrate until the gong sounded again. The voice once more paid homage to the leader. I learned that this happened three times each day. The gong sounded at 8:00 a.m., 2:00 p.m., and 8:00 p.m.

As before, I remained standing during the worship. After everyone had arisen, we took a short walk down the avenue and entered another building. The sign at the lower landing read "Visitor Home." We went through a door that also opened into the wall in four directions. Except for a human-looking robot, I was alone in what amounted to a very large mansion. Instead of regular windows, though, there were these amazing lit stained glass 3D scenes of mountains, lakes, valleys, and oceans on all the walls.

The robot who, like the militia men, could float low over the stylish wood floors, immediately escorted me to use what I soon recognized as a bathroom. I might have been at a loss had the robot not shown me directions on a handheld computer-type device for how to use the facilities. I soon received my own such device to use. It even answered any spoken questions I asked it. The directions showed how to use the suction toilets that came out of the wall to take care of the more serious elimination business, and there were both urinals for men and women for the liquid waste. It was clear that the women used the larger cups and men the smaller. The toilets and cups automatically sanitized after each use. Nice. And so interesting to see women finally getting the same convenience men had had for years. That sure would have shortened long lines in front of the public restroom stalls from my world!

I was surprised to see, and declined use of, a booth that had the familiar headset and my choice of five experiences I could dial into. I could have experienced an earthquake, Rio carnival parade, sunset walk, sunrise walk, or rodeo bull ride. “No, thank you,” I said aloud toward the device.

I looked around for something that might be a TV or a device that had movies on it but found nothing. When I asked the robot and the handheld about this matter, both had no idea what I was talking about. There was a history of how the Beast saved the world, however, which I did watch on the handheld device. It was a propaganda documentary about how that individual arose after the Great War to save “a lost and ravaged world and to restore it to health.”

I had a dinner that evening. On a wall screen in what turned out to be my guest bedroom, I used a penlike wand to point to a checkbox next to food pictures to order exactly what I wanted. I chose what appeared to be lasagna with bread, a carrot and spinach-looking quiche, an apple, and what tasted like lemon sparkling water. As I ate at a chair with an armrest table, I heard more of the familiar chime music playing that I had heard in the cushion bench. I finished my food. But where were the desserts? None to be found! No wonder everyone was so skinny!

After dinner, I used one of the highlight treats in the visitor home, an automatic shower! I was directed by the robot to stand in the center of a room about ten-by-ten-feet wide, naked, of course. Laser lights showed up all over me, clearly directing the mechanized arms that came out of the walls holding wet, soapy sponges, to scrub me down. Hot air filled the room and a giant spray of warm water rinsed me off. As I left, all the wetness in the room was sucked out and evaporated. I have to get one of those showers for my apartment back in my world. I wonder if the handheld device can set me up with a time tunnel delivery!

It was not hard for me to go to sleep on the comfy bed that came out of a hidden compartment in the wall. It even arrived with a stand that unfolded, along with a small light. I put the hand-held device on the stand. With the arrival of the bed, there again was that same chime music. It seemed to come out of the wall. I quickly drifted off. As I faded, I asked God to watch over me, to give me the wisdom to understand what I was living through, and would He please show me the reason I was brought to Alumina. And I gave a definite amen to that!

An intermittent buzzing woke me up. It was coming from the hand-held on the stand.

"I have to get up already? I'm still tired!" I yelled this at the handheld, then reached over to grab it. The buzzing stopped as soon as I touched the device.

"Good! I can turn this thing off." As I looked to set the gadget back down, I noticed my name on the screen. It read below it that I should touch the round blue screen icon for a message. I did so, and there again was a mysterious note.

"David. Leave the visitor home now. No one will stop you. There is no city life at night. The citizens are all in hibernation trance mode.

"Go to the building lobby and walk out the main doors. Even after the militia awaken, they will not be able to track you. You have no mark. With no one to use them, there are very few avenue or building lights at night. Take care as you walk. Follow the avenue to where the sun set earlier. We will meet you there. Go now. We are friends who wish to help you."

"Well, I have no reason not to trust these mysterious people. How they know who I am and where I am all the time, I have no clue. But I will do what they say. Here goes."

I sure hoped that I could finally meet these people! In no time, I had passed through the main lobby doors and was out on the street. Just as the message said, no one was around and everything was rather dark. I got my bearings and headed down the avenue at the end of which I had seen the sun setting. So far, so good.

It might have been an hour walk until I arrived at the city border. A sign warned me in capital letters not to go no farther, with a promise of electrocution if I did! I sure did not need that, especially if it might draw attention to myself. There was a very nice park there, much larger than the one I had seen in the headquarters building, but also with a stream and rainbow bridge. And there were more cushion benches. And I had the urge to wait on one.

"So now what?" I said out loud as I walked over to one of the benches. I looked up at the light from the stars and the moon above, both shining through the city dome.

"Yes. So now what?" I was just lowering myself to sit down in the cushy park bench and maybe enjoy more of the chimes music, even possibly drift off into a nap until friends arrived to help me, when I bolted upright out of sheer panic. "Ahh! What was I thinking? Yes, they can't track me because I don't have the mark, but they were able to find me before in the bench because I didn't have it! That is all I need! For the system to locate me out here, just when I may be finally free of the spying eyes. I am a fugitive. I am supposed to be under escort outside the visitor home. I had walked to the city border with no trouble. The city was, in fact, asleep, just as the note had promised. It would be my own fault to be found now, to sit down and be discovered again. Reality check!"

I was breathing heavily as I looked around for someplace else safe to rest. There was some nice grass behind the bench where I could be unseen, relaxed, and remain anonymous. As I lay down, several favorite Bible verses came to mind. I sure could use them now to get myself together and calm. It was great to think that someone greater than I am might be controlling my life, especially now in this stranger than strange reality.

"Let's see. I can sure use Romans 8:28. 'We know that in all things God works for good with those who love him, who are called according to His purpose.' I don't know His purpose in all of this, but I am sure that there is one. Maybe it has to do with my last prayer in Pittsburgh, to know that He is there for sure. Finding an end-times anti-Christ type leader of the world exactly as Revelation describes him, including the part where everyone is required to have the mark of the Beast, and another leader dedicated to him described both here and in the Bible as a dragon, sure is convincing!

"And Proverbs 3:5–6. 'Trust in the Lord with all your heart. Depend not upon your own understanding. In all your ways acknowledge Him, and He will make straight your path.' I remembered a psalm too, one my third-grade teacher used to recite every morning as we began the school day. It must have been her favorite. I had heard it so often I had it memorized by the end of the school year. The twenty-third Psalm.

'The Lord is my shepherd, I shall not want;
'He makes me to lie down in green pastures.
'He leads me beside still waters;
'He restores my soul.'"

That was all I needed. I was still tired from my walk. And with the sound of waters somewhere nearby, perhaps under a rainbow bridge in the park, and with me lying comfortably now in what amounted to a warm green pasture in that park, I soon drifted off to sleep.

Life Chapter 5

At Last!

"David! Get up! We need to go!"

"Go away. I need to sleep," I replied.

"We sent you the directions. We are friends. We must leave!" At last! The people behind the mystery messages!

Sure enough. There was a small group of men standing there as I lay in the warm grass. They were looking down at me, then off to all sides as if worried about being seen. I instinctively went to brush myself off. I was completely dry. What a benefit having the dome. There was no wet grass from night dew and no leaves blowing around! It was still dark, but I could tell that I had gotten in a much-needed nap.

"Follow us!" I was ready to but hesitated when I noticed that these men had on the exact same uniforms that the city militia who had escorted me inside headquarters and the visitor center had worn. But when I made out the tanned tone of their skins in the moonlight, I was put at ease and followed, as ordered. I figured they must have had on the same uniforms to pass as the good guys if seen from a distance.

But where were we going? We were already at the dome edge. Could they have a way of moving through the domed city wall? We walked along the boundary for only about fifty yards when two of them stopped and looked back to the city for a moment. Then they bent over to lift up about a six-feet-by-six-feet chunk of grass that rested on an attached platform of the same size. Lifting it revealed a large hole beneath. I could hardly believe it as we climbed down a ladder. Lights came on automatically. I looked up from what turned out to be a small room to see the last fellow pulling down what was clearly a grass trap door above and joining us.

"We'll explain things later, David. Right now, we need to get out of here and through the valley before the city begins to wake up and you are found missing. I am so glad we were able to hike in and to arrive in time after we sent that last message. We had no idea what fate the enforcer might decide for you. He thankfully decided to give you a chance to join them. We appreciate you following our directions. And I am so glad we found you so close to our secret entrance. Please join us in prayer."

I bowed my head with the others. "Lord, thank you that David is well and that we are now able to guide him to safety. Please help us in a situation similar to what a young shepherd boy of the same name was also facing when he wrote the twenty-third Psalm, 'The Lord is my shepherd, I shall not want. He leads me in the paths of righteousness for His name's sake. Even though I walk through the valley of the shadow of death, I will fear no evil. Surely goodness and mercy shall follow me all the days of my life; and I shall dwell in the house of the Lord forever.'"

Ironic that this stranger should be using the very psalm I used a part of to go to sleep this very night, and also ironic that he left out the part I could have used just hours ago as I ate my lasagna dinner in the visitor center: "Thou preparest a table before me in the presence of mine enemies."

"David, it is extremely important that you follow us in line. There are still old mines planted in this valley from just after the Great War to keep intruders away as the city was being built, and we have the handheld device that shows us where they are located. Not all are still active, but we don't have the time to worry about which ones are live. Also, it will be a bit chilly compared to the set temperature inside the city dome, but your body heat will build up inside your clothing as you walk, and you should be fine in a few minutes. We are in the region of what was once Flagstaff, Arizona.

It is summer. It is only chilly at night, in the 50s this time of year. It will soon warm up considerably after sunrise, probably into the 80s. The shoes you have on should be fine. They got you through the city streets of Pittsburgh and out to the dome boundary from the center of Alumina. They will serve well here too."

"Got it," I responded to the fellow who did all the talking, whom I concluded must be the team leader. "I will follow everyone else in a line through the valley, and I should not be worried about the temperature or my shoes. How did you know about me being in Pittsburgh?"

The fellow gave a quick reply as we went from one side of the room to the other, "You will know everything in due time."

We climbed up another ladder, ascending through a trap door identical to the first, only we ended up on the surface on the other side of the city dome wall. The top of this door did not have grass, but resembled the stonier ground where we came out. One man carefully replaced the hatch in the ground and, so that the door's location was hidden, smoothed the lines out with a branch lying there. He then used the same branch to smooth over the tracks behind us as we moved into a line and began to march away from the city and into the valley. I was placed third in the line of the four of us. After about a hundred yards, the man with the branch tossed it to the side and remained in line behind me. The fellow in front with the handheld was being careful to walk in a certain path, altering our direction every so often. We even occasionally entered a stream that flowed alongside us. I soon adjusted to my wet, cold shoes. I was startled occasionally when fish jumped out of the water and when frogs croaked from the sand and then splashed in.

About two hours later by my watch, which I knew by experience would mean about six miles walking, the sun was rising behind us, and we had made it a good way through the valley. The men suddenly stopped and looked around. Seeming to be satisfied, the fellow in front put away the guiding device, and we walked over behind a large boulder and began to walk up a path on the side of the mountain. It was somewhat overgrown, but passable. We continued all the way to the top.

The sun had become much brighter as we ascended. I noticed the breathtaking scenery of red rock formations. We reached the top and began to walk into the woods there, losing sight of the grandeur of the rock displays we left behind. I felt a closeness to God as I noticed how the trees seemed to be raising their branches heavenward in praise of the Creator of this world. Suddenly, a small village under the trees appeared. A group of about twenty people was huddling around a fire. They had blankets wrapped around them. There were many one-story wooden buildings here and there.

The group jumped up when they saw our approach and ran over, variously saying excitedly, "Aaron! You're back!"

"John! Frank! Welcome home!"

"Thank God you're safe!"

"You found David!"

"Was there any trouble?

There were many hugs. The leader who was identified as Aaron was the first to speak, "Do we ever have trouble in the city at night? They are much too trusting. I doubt that they even have their sensors or viewers on. They must conclude that our fear of their previous robot attacks just after we decided to leave the city will keep us away."

Then I could not believe my eyes! There in the group was the face of the girl I had helped in Pittsburgh, the one who had been attacked and stabbed! No way! She had made eye contact and was coming toward me with a big smile.

I called out as I pointed to her, "It's you! I can't believe it. It's you. You are okay!"

She came over to me and hugged me as one in the crowd added, "This is Martha. She is one of us."

"But…but…" I was so confused. One of them?

Aaron added, "You will know all in due time. Thanks to everyone for waiting up for us. Let's offer up a word of thanks and then get some rest. Pastor? Will you give us our daily devotion early today?"

Everyone joined hands and looked over to an older fellow. He nodded his agreement and said, "Gladly." They all then bowed their heads. He spoke, "I chose parts of Psalm 90 for our daily reflection. It seems appropriate for the Great War we survived with the Lord's help a few years back, for our life here in the wilderness as God's people, and for the time travel we have been doing of late using the city transporter that brought David to us. Let us hear these words then from Psalm 90, 'Lord, thou hast been our dwelling place in all generations. Before the mountains were brought forth, or ever thou hadst formed the earth and the world, from everlasting to everlasting, thou art God. Thou turnest man to destruction; and sayest, "Return, O children of men." For a thousand years in thy sight are but as yesterday when it is past, and as a watch in the night. We spend our years as a tale that is told. So teach us to number our days, so that we may get a heart of wisdom. Satisfy us in the morning with thy steadfast love; that we may rejoice and be glad all our days. Make us glad as many days as thou hast afflicted us, and as many years as we have seen evil. Let thy work appear unto thy servants, and thy glorious power to their children. Let the favor of the Lord our God be upon us, and establish thou the work of our hands upon us, yea the works of thy hands establish thou it.' Lord, thank you for this word whose truth never changes, even as you are eternal, and thank you for your protection for those who went to the city this night. Finally, we acknowledge your continued blessings in our lives, knowing that you are God. We commend ourselves into your hands, Father. Amen."

There was a loud communal amen in response, and I was lead inside one of the wood buildings and given what appeared to be a homemade blanket folded several times to sleep on, another blanket to cover myself with, and a pillow of the same cloth the blankets were made of, stuffed with what I was told were feathers. I was very comfortable as I took an open spot on the wooden floor on my blanket and lay down.

I had a lot of questions on my mind, including how the girl I had tried to help as she was attacked in Pittsburgh got here. I was so thankful to see her completely well! Other questions occurred to me too, but I found they made little difference in me going fast to sleep. I had come a long way in a few hours, a long way from danger when I escaped from downtown Alumina as the citizens slept, when I hid from the city authorities in the park, and when I finally found friends hidden in the nearby wilderness.

Life Chapter 6

The Truth

Martha was waiting for me outside the hut when I woke up. She was chatting with an older woman who was introduced as Ruth. They both showed me how they used a type of sanitizer with a bowl of water to wash most mornings, only sometimes going to the spring pool nearby to soak completely or to take a shower when it rained. They pointed to a separate wash building and I entered on the men's side, washed using the sanitizer, then met the two women again after. We three had breakfast together. It included a tasty sort of oatmeal with fresh berries and tea to wash it down. Martha explained that all the single girls had chaperones when with single men, so that is why Ruth was with us. It was part of the life routine. Martha told me that Ruth means "friend and companion" in Hebrew and that Ruth fit her name as she had always been a good friend to her since they had met during the Great War.

They called themselves the Fishnet and used the fish symbol as their insignia. There were parts of branches from bushes hanging around the village tied into fishlike shapes. Martha spoke first, "David, you must be filled with questions. What do you want to know?"

"Yes, thank you, Martha. I have tons of questions. Where should I start? Okay. First, what were you doing in Pittsburgh if you are from here? And when I left you, you had just been stabbed. How did you get well so soon, or for that matter, at all?"

"Fair enough. I will do my best for you. Okay. Here goes. Ruth, please add anything important that I leave out." Ruth nodded her agreement. "Where you are now is well into the future of earth by several hundred years. I was born in this area, which was Flagstaff, Arizona. We don't have schools any more like you did when you lived. Our parents saw that we followed the public dictates as we were educated on what was called the Social World Record. It was on a screen like your computers. After your generation, the world became a lawless mess, especially in the Middle East when from all sides, including from the north, countries came against Israel. Robots became the police so as not to endanger the lives of humans. But the lawlessness got out of control everywhere. It was like how God's people behaved in the wilderness with the golden calf. People gave in to what came natural, like sensuousness, anger, jealousy, and greed. You name the negative human motivations, they showed it. This lead to what we call the Great War, where nations suddenly began attacking one another with nuclear incineration."

"Nuclear incineration?" I asked.

Ruth clarified, "Orbiting war satellites would pinpoint what they considered enemy targets, and their storage systems would deliver nuclear missiles to those locations. These would explode in midair, about a mile overhead and incinerate everything above ground within a one-hundred-mile radius. Radiation would remain deadly for two weeks. So many were caught by surprise everywhere in the beginning that few got into shelters and escaped the deadly blasts. We here in Flagstaff did not take a direct hit and were protected somewhat by the mountains. We had more time to get below ground to safety. The Phoenix area, south of here, was hit badly. We were almost exactly one hundred miles away from them. All major cities throughout the world were hit hard. What else, Martha?"

Martha continued, "After the war, we few survivors became part of the nearby Alumina building project and lived there. This project was one of ten cities for the few survivors left around the world. It was organized by the men you know as the Beast and the Dragon. Building cities is much more automatic and advanced than in your world. At first, we did not know who had taken control of things but were glad to go along with any plans if it meant being provided with the necessaries of life. Soon a communication system introduced us to the two men who presented themselves as the saviors of the world."

Ruth joined in again. "Believe it or not, if you know the Book of Daniel or Revelation in the Holy Bible, you will know who these two are." She read from a handheld. "Listen to this from chapter 13 of the Book of Revelation and tell me if anything sounds familiar, 'Now the Beast which I saw was like a leopard, his feet were like the feet of a bear, and his mouth like the mouth of a lion. The dragon gave him his power, his throne, and great authority. And I saw one of his heads as if it had been mortally wounded, and his deadly wound was healed. And all the world marveled and followed the Beast. So they worshiped the Dragon who gave authority to the Beast; and they worshiped the Beast, saying, "Who *is* like the Beast? Who is able to make war with him?" And he was given a mouth speaking great things and blasphemies, and he was given authority to continue for forty-two months. Then he opened his mouth in blasphemy against God, to blaspheme His name, His tabernacle, and those who dwell in heaven. It was granted to him to make war with the saints and to overcome them. And authority was given him over every tribe, tongue, and nation. All who dwell on the earth will worship him, whose names have not been written in the Book of Life of the Lamb slain from the foundation of the world. If anyone has an ear, let him hear. He who leads into captivity shall go into captivity; he who kills with the sword must be killed with the sword. Here is the patience and the faith of the saints. Then I saw another beast coming up out of the earth, and he had two horns like a lamb and spoke like a dragon. And he exercises all the authority of the first beast in his presence, and causes the earth and those who dwell in it to worship the first beast, whose deadly wound was healed. He performs great signs, so that he even makes fire come down from heaven on the earth in the sight of men. And he deceives those who dwell on the earth by those signs which he was granted to do in the sight of the Beast, telling those who dwell on the earth to make an image to the Beast who was wounded by the sword and lived. He was granted *power* to give breath to the image of the Beast, that the image of the Beast should both speak and cause as many as would not worship the image of the Beast to be killed. He causes all, both small and great, rich and poor, free and slave, to receive a mark on their right hand or on their foreheads, and that no one may buy or sell except one who has the mark or the name of the Beast, or the number of his name. Here is wisdom. Let him who has understanding calculate the number of the Beast, for it is the number of a man: His number is 666.'"

"Ruth! Stop right there. That is it! That is what I thought was in the Bible when I saw it happening! The citizens of Alumina all had to have that mark of the Beast! I saw those marks, just where it said they would be, on the foreheads or on their hands. And all the marks started with 666, just like it says there! And I talked during my hearing in court to the one they called the Dragon, the enforcer. And all the people would show their marks and publicly bow down to the Beast when the announcement was made. Wow! That is completely scary! And where does you living out here fit into all this?"

Martha took over. "As I said, we continued to live in the city after it was built and as the world recovered from the Great War. When we realized who the Beast really was, we chose to leave. That was two years ago. I was still a girl, twelve when the war happened, fifteen when we left, and nineteen now. Ruth? You are older and understood more then. Tell about the Beast."

Ruth, who looked to be about forty, did just that. "The change came the day the Beast broadcasted his visit to the Holyland, which is the first city of the ten he oversaw the construction of around the world. Alumina is the seventh. I do give him credit for leading us out of the rubble after the devastating nuclear Holocaust. There were so few who emerged after the two-week radiation quarantine. He was known as Lyle Crawford up until we left. His ego slowly grew from very important world figure to thinking he was god. He made contact with those left on the planet, encouraged us through the black rains and weather upheavals as earth balanced its atmosphere after the attacks, and had an amazing crew of robots and advanced technology that all originated in his legendary scientific laboratory in Germany that survived the war. And with them, he built the ten cities. Notice in the Bible passage I read that it is the Dragon who gives power to the Beast. The Dragon, who as you said is also known as the enforcer, is actually Satan himself. He gives power and authority to his representative, the Beast, who is his puppet. The Beast was actually assassinated in the Holyland city when he arrived there! We saw the live feed and the reports after. They left his body for several days on the steps where he was shot. And just as it mentions recovering from a mortal wound in that Bible passage, so he did. He suddenly stood up and lived again. He demonstrated power by reaching up both arms as he blasphemed God's name. And when he ordered lightning and thunder to come down around him, it did. He then dramatically went into the Holy of Holies in the Jewish Temple and declared himself god. Martha? You saw all this."

"Yes. I won't go into the war itself for now and exactly who did what. That is a story worthy of an entire book. But I will say that most countries were wiped completely out by surprise in the beginning. Turns out that the Beast instigated it so he could take control of the world. He initiated widespread, preplanned attacks, and the nations hit blindly sent out retaliatory strikes, thinking it was other countries attacking them.

"Asia is the only domed city for what was once the most populated area of earth. That region was completely unprotected from the attacks. The antidelivery measures of the United States prevented it from being a total casualty, so it was left with the most people, so also with the most cities now on earth. New York and Los Angeles were among those hardest hit.

"American domed cities include Metro, in what was once Pittsburgh, Atland, in what was once Atlanta, in the popular Southeast, and Alumina here in the Southwest. North of here, in what was once Canada, is Vanco, which was Vancouver. In order of their numbers, one to ten, then, the world's cities are number one Holyland, once Jerusalem, Egypto, once Cairo, Euro, once Berlin, Asia, once Hong Kong, Aussie, one time Sydney, Somera, once Buenos Aires in Argentina, our Alumina is the seventh, Vanco eighth, Metro ninth, and number ten, Atland. Ruth? Tell about the leader and why we fled."

"After he arose from the dead—and we know now that Satan was responsible for that miracle—power got to Mr. Crawford's ego, and he knew the world was his to do with as he decided. As I mentioned, he soon broadcast a special event from where he was in the first city, Holyland. Of course, everyone tuned in. He stood in the Holy of Holies in the temple and proclaimed himself the long-awaited coming of the messiah who would continue to save the world. He used verses from the Bible to declare that he was god. We later confirmed many prophetic warnings about such claims. Matthew 24:24 reads, 'For false christs and false prophets will arise and perform great signs and wonders, so as to lead astray, if possible, even the elect.' Crawford showed many technological wonders to entice us to continue to follow him. He offered security, food, shelter, and health equipment. That is when he declared that he should thereafter be referred to as the Beast and explained how everyone who wished to remain in the cities had to have his mark to do business. You asked about how Martha got well. He provided what was once a one-of-a-kind healing machine for each city. This machine, called a Healioport, is a computer that can think. It uses a headset like those in the EmoteArama booths. If someone puts it on, the machine can scan that person's body and assess human disease and injury and guide the human body, the brain itself, to heal the body overnight while the patient sits in a chair. Each city has one. The team brought you through the Alumina time transporter and took you and Martha to the machine in that city for healing.

"That was at night when no one was around. After your healings, Martha returned with us to the wilderness village, but our team took you over to the EmoteArama when the city was about to wake up and left you in the arena booth so you could see firsthand what life was like here now. Martha had gone through to Pittsburgh in your time to get supplies for us that the city could not provide. The team saw what happened on their handhelds. Speaking of handhelds, listen to this passage in mine about what Jesus said in Matthew 24:15–16 when asked what his disciples should look for when he returned again. He warned, 'So when you see the abomination of desolation spoken of by the prophet Daniel, standing in the holy place [let the reader understand], then let those who are in Judea flee to the mountains.' Well, we from our city and others from theirs did flee. We, in fact, literally did flee to the mountains, just as Jesus advised in his warning. We fled that same day that Crawford announced that he was the Beast and that his enforcer would be the Dragon." Ruth paused and took a deep breath. "I think we could all sure use a break now." Both Martha and I nodded our agreement.

"But listen to one more short passage before we rest. This is Paul speaking from the second chapter of 2 Thessalonians. 'Now concerning the coming of our Lord Jesus Christ and our assembling to meet him, we beg you, brethren, not to be quickly shaken in mind or excited, either by spirit or by word, or by letter purporting to be from us, to the effect that the day of the Lord has come. Let no one deceive you in any way; for that day will not come, unless the rebellion comes first, and the man of lawlessness is revealed, the son of perdition, who opposes and exalts himself against every so-called god or object of worship, so that he takes his seat in the temple of God, proclaiming himself to be God. Do you not remember that when I was still with you I told you this? And you know what is restraining him now so that he may be revealed in his time. For the mystery of lawlessness is already at work; only he who now restrains it will do so until he is out of the way. And then the lawless one will be revealed, and the Lord Jesus will slay him with the breath of his mouth and destroy him by his appearing and his coming. The coming of the lawless one by the activity of Satan will be with all power and with pretended signs and wonders, and with all wicked deception for those who are to perish, because they refused to love the truth and so be saved. Therefore God sends upon them a strong delusion, to make them believe what is false, so that all may be condemned who did not believe the truth but had pleasure in unrighteousness.'"

Despite my fatigue, I could not hold in my excitement. "Wow! This is amazing! You are seeing the end-times. What I saw and what you just told me happened are Bible prophecy right in front of us, right out of the Book of books!"

Ruth added, "And the encouraging thing is that this all has a happy ending because Jesus returns to create a new heaven and a new earth and to reign in peace and love for a thousand years."

"But," Martha added, "there are other passages that mention that followers of Jesus might suffer and die when they refuse to worship the Beast and his image. That is a not so nice thought. That means people like us."

"Well," I concluded, "this is all amazing to learn about. I finally have a clue about what is going on here! But honestly, where do I fit into all of this? What happens to me now? Must I return to Pittsburgh and live there again? Do I stay here and live in your village? What next?"

Life Chapter 7

What Next?

Both Martha and Ruth grew quiet. Martha looked especially sad, for some reason, almost near tears. Ruth looked over at her understandingly and finally spoke, looking back at me. "Yes, what, in fact, is next for you? What are your options now, David? That is some big question for your life. Tell you what. We must meet with Aaron to get his answer on that. He has a gift of wisdom, of common sense, that we all depend upon here. Let me see if he is around and can talk. I'll be right back."

"Thank you, Ruth," I encouraged.

I followed her with my eyes as she walked across the village. Soon she was standing outside one of the shacks with someone and was waving us over. We went immediately. It was, in fact, Aaron, and the pastor emerged, too, bringing out enough rope and branch chairs for us to use. We were all soon seated and relaxing in the shade. Aaron started things off.

"So, David, I understand you asked about what might be next for you and that you would like to hear my view. I see several possible options."

"Thanks. It would be good to know what my choices are now and which one is most realistic and promising for me and what isn't. If you had told me five days ago in Pittsburgh what was about to happen to me, I would have told you to write the story up and offer it to the Sunday funny papers or maybe give it to a science fiction publisher."

Aaron smiled. "Pastor, will you lift this issue up in prayer?"

"Yes. Let's please have a few moments of quiet time to begin to focus on the issue at hand for David." A minute or so passed. There was a light breeze blowing through the trees, some distant villager talk, some laughter, and birds singing. "Lord, please give David the wisdom and direction he needs to decide his future. Thank you for loving us and being there for us. Direct our paths ever to walk with you. Amen. Aaron? What are David's options, as you see them?"

"Okay. I see several possibilities. First, David can remain here with us and be a part of our wilderness community. He is certainly welcome to join us as a brother in the Lord. He might soon accept one of the service jobs. We can sure use workers. Looking down the road, he might marry one of the members and raise a family. However, his risks are the same as ours. Those drawbacks are having to face the danger, uncertainty, and annoyance of the elements, having to provide for ourselves and being vulnerable to inevitable shortages, possible capture, torture, and death at the hands of the Alumina Militia, and hoping to occasionally use the city resources for our needs and interests. Second, David is certainly free to return to the city of Alumina, to give his allegiance to the Beast, to accept his mark, and to live there in relative comfort and security, though maybe not at mental ease while having to worship a dictator regularly, and not really having a life of his own. Someone would always be watching him. Finally, a third option is that we could hope one night to get David back into the city, back to the time transporter, and back to his time and life in Pittsburgh. Well, I see those three options. Does anyone see any others?"

"I would like to add one more possibility for myself for general consideration."

"Certainly, David. What do you have?"

"I thought I might like to live in the Holyland City, in Jerusalem, to see Bible prophecy unfold firsthand. The Dragon did say that I could become a citizen of any city. How many in history would have given anything to be there and to be such a witness? But that could mean my present life would shorten if the Lord returns soon. And from what I see happening, that could be any day now. Another negative is that I could be discovered as a believer and killed and maybe never see the fulfillment of prophecy. A plus is that living in what was Jerusalem could mean watching the actual promised Lord's triumphant return, witness Him give Satan what he deserves, and living in the thousand-year world peace Jesus institutes to fulfill prophecy. Then there is eternal life in heaven to follow."

"I had not thought of that fourth option," Aaron admitted. "And again, being martyred is a possibility no matter what your choice is—that is, if you decide to remain in this time and place. If we can get you back to Pittsburgh before the attack on Martha, at least you can avoid being punished in your time for a crime you did not commit. We can then help Martha instead of you having to step in to rescue her, and you could avoid this entire visit but still be aware of all that happened because memories are not erased after time travel experiences."

"This was good sitting down with all of you to look at the possibilities for me. I do now see a clear answer here."

"It is good you have a sure idea of your future," Aaron encouraged. What is your decision? We will help in any way we can."

"Thank you. I already went to Israel with my family, to the Holy Land, to Jerusalem, on what they called a trip of a lifetime. They were right. It was. That trip becomes even more meaningful as I grow older. And I would rather remember it that way, as it was, not ruined by some gigantic domed city built over it or by what the Beast said and did there. As I think about it, that would ruin it for me. Just knowing that Jesus will have the victory in the end over evil and darkness is enough for me. No, I think it would be best to return to my time, to my life in Pittsburgh, to the life I know, to the world where God put me. This was amazing being able to see the future. Before all this happened, I was having a spiritual crisis, wondering if God was really there. I had prayed for Him to show me that He existed for sure. You have to agree that what happened to me is convincing. I realize how real God is now, especially because of your example as his faithful remnant living here in defiance of a city that does not honor our Lord and promises death to believers who do not show allegiance to the anti-Christ. Also, I saw prophecy being fulfilled right in front of my eyes. I learned how truly "living and active" the Word of God is, as it says in Hebrews. I would now like to see what God has planned for me in my world. No matter what I decided, as it says in Scripture, 'God is the same yesterday, today and forever.' And He would be with me no matter my decision.'"

"Ironic, isn't it?" offered Aaron. "You are one of the few who ever lived who would know that God is the same yesterday, today, and forever. After your return, you will have literally seen all three. You will have visited all three dimensions."

The pastor got up from his chair saying, "Amen to that brother. Well said. So we have a decision! This is exciting. We helped a brother to decide his very future. Anyone else want to offer anything?" No one did. "Then let's pray for this fellow and that future."

They each laid a hand on my shoulders, and each spoke a prayer for me. After the amen, Martha rushed away in much distress.

"Martha!" I called after her. "Thank you, everyone. I really appreciate what you did for me. I have to find out what's going on with Martha. She seems really upset." I soon caught up to her. She was sobbing, kneeling behind some bushes just outside the village. I waited for her to finish what was clearly a prayer. I heard her say in the end, "Father, thy will be done. As your son Jesus trusted you, so do I. Into thy hands I commend my future." She finally looked over at me.

"Hello, David." She was wiping tears from her eyes with the sleeves of her blouse and looking much relieved.

"Martha. What is it? Are you okay? Why were you so upset? What's going on?"

"I'm not sure how to say this. Maybe I should just come right out with it."

"To be honest with you, I hope you were upset for the same reason I am feeling unsettled too."

"What reason is that?"

"Well, this may seem to be coming out of nowhere. I once promised God when I was a little boy, after telling a lie and feeling so badly about it, that I would always be honest and open about things from then on. So I will be now, for sure. Here goes. Martha, I can't express to you the love I've felt for you. I mean, I had just met you. But when I saw you again here, that you were still alive and how happy you were to see me, I've had this very special feeling overwhelming me for you, like I need to be near you all the time, like I want to hold you in my arms forever, like we were chosen for each other by God long before we met. These moments alone with you yesterday and today—well, as alone with you as possible with Ruth around, anyway—have been very special for me. If you feel the same way about me as I do for you, I am hoping that you are as upset about me leaving and maybe never seeing me again, as I am about that same very real possibility, that I would be leaving you and might never see you again either."

A big smile replaced Martha's sad face. "You really love me that much?"

"I do, Martha, a deeper love than I've ever felt for any woman before ever."

"Yes! Yes! I was upset because you were going away! I have come to love you so quickly, so much! You risked your life for me in Pittsburgh! You are a rare, special man. I have loved being alone with you too!"

We hugged for a long time, then our first kiss. Soon we heard Ruth a short way off calling out for where Martha was.

"Over here, Ruth!" Ruth soon appeared.

"Hello, you two." She smiled. Then she added in a playful voice, "Off on your own, I see. I'm telling the pastor. You two have been naughty going off by yourselves. You know the rules." We all laughed. "Anything I should know?"

I spoke up, "Could you please give us just five minutes more alone? I promise that we will not be up to anything we shouldn't be. There is one more thing we need to settle."

"I don't see how five more minutes will hurt. Yes. Meet me at my hut when you are done."

Ruth left, and I was left staring into Martha's teary, happy eyes and smiling face. I looked down, broke off a blade of grass, tied it into a round shape, and knelt down in front of her.

"Martha, daughter of the living God, and in a wonderfully new way I don't understand yet, new love of my life, will you marry me?" I offered the grass ring.

"Are you sure, David?"

"I was never so sure of anything in my life. And I don't even know why. That's the scary part. But I love you more than life itself. It is a genuine love from God."

Martha added, "I love you too, David. Yes. Yes! My answer is yes!" She put out her hand to accept the grass ring. I slid it onto her ring finger as she exclaimed, "I can't believe this is happening! I am so happy!" We hugged and kissed again. As I held her in my arms, I added, "Lord, bless this union in thy sight, and may we be ever mindful of you and the happiness you bring to us if we will only trust in you with all our hearts. Thank you that you are God, that you are love, and that we are made in your image, that you gave us such moments as this to share the love in our hearts you gave us."

"Wow! That may have been the most beautiful prayer I ever heard, right from your heart! I wish everyone could have heard that."

"Yes. That came right from my heart to yours, Martha."

We hugged and kissed again, then went to find Ruth so that she could be the first to know the good news.

I must say, they certainly did not waste any time at Fishnet. That night, there was singing and dancing after everyone heard the news of our engagement. And believe it or not, the night's celebration was climaxed with our wedding ceremony, yes, then and there. Martha wore a beautiful white robe with a branch fish crown of many colored flowers in her flowing hair. We were then escorted to one of the buildings which we had to ourselves for one blissful honeymoon night.

There was more singing and dancing the next day. It was one of the happiest moments of my life. Soon, however, Martha and I understood the reason for the serious look on Aaron's face as he approached us as the afternoon celebration came to an end. Somehow we knew what was on his mind.

"It's time. Tonight is as good as any other. Let's not put this off. Let's get you two back to Pittsburgh to start a new life together. You haven't changed your mind, have you, David?"

"No, Aaron. I am ready."

"And you, Martha, you will return to Pittsburgh with David too?"

"I could never leave my husband, the new love of my life, willingly. Yes. I will go too. No question."

Aaron nodded to the pastor, who called everyone together and made an announcement about our return that night. There were tears, laughter, and well-wishes.

After final heartfelt goodbyes, Martha and I were soon following the same team down the mountain who had brought me up. I was sad I could not see those grand red rock colors in the formations again at night, but they were still worth seeing, black silhouettes standing majestically against the moonlit sky. I promised Martha that we would have a true honeymoon in Flagstaff after we got back to Pittsburgh. She smiled and stopped me to hug me.

We made it back into the city through the secret underground room and back through the time transporter without incident. The team gave us hugs just before we entered the green mist of the tunnel. I do hope that they made it back to their village safely. That is the last time we expected that we would see any of the faithful of Fishnet, or anyone at all from that era, for that matter. We returned to a date and time before the park attack took place, thereby avoiding a rift in time and any repercussions that such an alteration might have had on the future.

So there you have my story. As I said, Martha and I arrived back in the Pittsburgh park before the time we had left, before she was attacked. The next day she wanted to spend with me in the Museum of Natural History. What a delight to have her in my life. There were a few awkward moments explaining to my friends and family how we were suddenly married. But no one seemed to suspect anything because of our true and sudden love for one another. There could be no denying that when you saw how we looked into each other's eyes and hugged so often. Anyway, after that first museum trip, Martha had a real treat. You see, that first day back, I introduced her to fast food! And Pittsburgh had plenty of that to go around!

As I passed that statue of Galileo during our day together, I had new and deeper insight into the world, into my life. I shared with Martha about the spiritual crisis I had been in when I passed Galileo before. I hoped that that great philosopher had found the deep satisfaction in his life that I had found in mine.

Thanks for hearing me out, reader. That was the happy ending of my story. That was the decision I made for my life. But there is one thing left that is just as important. What about you? What about your life? Will you have the same happy ending? Do you know for certain that there is a God? Are you beyond spiritual crisis and in the loving arms of your creator? Do you realize the truth of John 3 where we are told that "For God so loved the world that he gave his only Son, that whoever believes in him should not perish but have eternal life"? Have you found that ultimate relationship, that love, that care "that passes all understanding, that keeps our hearts and minds in Christ Jesus"?

Martha and I didn't get to Flagstaff right away, but we did get there. How can I express how wonderful that was, how meaningful, how memorable? We went into the wilderness and walked where the village would be and remembered our brothers and sisters there, the good friends we had decided to leave behind. We remembered our special moment when we first shared our love there for one another. We realized that by our decision to return to the past, we had avoided the opportunity to witness the end-times, to see firsthand God's final great victory over evil in the world. But by doing so, we had more of a guarantee of time to invest in our love for one another and were able to relax in the Lord.

Before we left the woods, we read aloud a Bible passage we had since found, related to the mark of the Beast on the hands and foreheads of the Alumina citizens. We had not realized that what the enemy required was in blasphemous response to what God had asked of his chosen people. They were commanded in the sixth chapter of Deuteronomy, verses 4 to 8, to do some things with God's Holy Word. They were to teach it to their children, talk about it in their daily lives, write it on their house doorposts and gates, "And you shall tie them as a sign upon your hand, and you shall put them as a band around your forehead." On their hands and foreheads! That is exactly where the Antichrist required his blasphemous mark of the Beast sign! As if He were God, and his mark was the ultimate law!

Finally, we read the verse from Hebrews 13:8 and understood its meaning as few others in history may have, "Jesus Christ is the same yesterday and today and forever." For you who believe and who know Jesus, who is, as he said in John 14:6, the way, the truth, and the life, by whom no one goes to the Father but by him, I include this from Numbers 6: "The LORD bless you and keep you; The LORD make his face to shine upon you and be gracious to you: The LORD lift up his countenance upon you, and give you peace."

And from Martha and from me, for all those in the wilderness, enjoying God's creation on your own terms, as you continue to walk in the pathways of righteousness, as you lie by green pastures, and as you find rest beside the still waters, I leave you with this hope from Genesis 31: "The Lord watch between you and me, when we are absent one from the other." How I wish I could hear everyone in the Fishnet wilderness community add their united "amen!"

About the Author

David Monroe Barto received the 2017 Albert Nelson Marquis Who's Who Lifetime Achievement Award given to those who achieved career longevity and demonstrated unwavering excellence in their chosen fields. Mr. Barto's chosen fields were teacher, actor, musician, and park ranger.

He is best known for combining all four of those areas in his over one thousand Henry David Thoreau and John Wesley one-man shows throughout the United States and in England. For these, he was featured on radio and television specials and in newspapers, including *The New York Times.* He also had an account published in an educational journal of how he used acting in a creative way in the classroom and spoke about the same at a national convention of teachers. Most importantly in his life, David found a saving faith in Jesus Christ as his personal Lord and Savior at the age of fifteen. This led to several dramatic moments in his life.

www.ingramcontent.com/pod-product-compliance
Lightning Source LLC
Chambersburg PA
CBHW041146050525
26188CB00045B/1033
* 9 7 9 8 8 8 5 4 0 1 3 4 0 *